This book belongs to

BLESSED EDITH STEIN

DIANE GOODE'S

B·O·O·K O·F

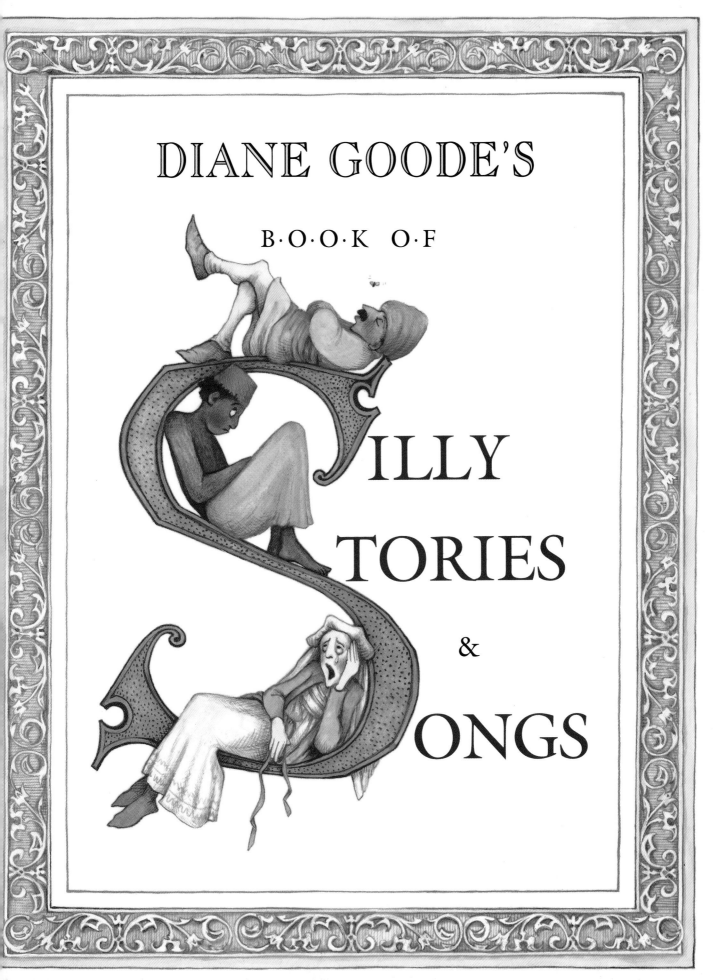

SILLY

STORIES

&

SONGS

DUTTON CHILDREN'S BOOKS NEW YORK

The publisher gratefully acknowledges permission to reprint on:

page 4, "Getting Common Sense," from *Anansi and Miss Lou,* by Louise Bennett. Reprinted by permission of Sangster's Book Stores Ltd., Kingston, Jamaica.

page 15, "A Lion Went for a Walk," from *Tomfoolery: Trickery and Foolery with Words,* by Alvin Schwartz, illustrated by Glen Rounds. Text copyright © 1973 by Alvin Schwartz. Selection reprinted by permission of HarperCollins Publishers.

page 17, "Get Up and Bar the Door," originally titled "There Are Such People," from *Noodlehead Stories from Around the World,* by M. A. Jagendorf. Copyright © 1957 by M. A. Jagendorf. Reprinted by permission of André Jagendorf and Merna Alpert.

page 21, "Bendemolena," copyright © 1967 by Ann G. Seidler and Janice B. Slepian. All rights reserved. Used with permission.

page 28, "Cuanto Le Gusta." By Ray Gilbert and Gabriel Ruiz. Copyright © 1940 by Promotora Hispano Americana de Musica, S.A. Copyright renewed. Copyright © 1948 by Peer International Corporation. Copyright renewed. Used by permission. All rights reserved.

page 31, "Talk," from *The Cow-Tail Switch,* by Harold Courlander and George Herzog. Copyright © 1947, 1975 by Harold Courlander. Reprinted by permission of Henry Holt and Company, Inc.

page 38, "On Top of Spaghetti," by Tom Glazer. Copyright © Songs Music, Inc., Scarborough, NY 10510. Reprinted by permission.

page 41, "Sweet Giongio," copyright © 1992 by Donna Jo Napoli. Reprinted by permission.

page 53, "The Disobedient Eels," from *The Disobedient Eels and Other Italian Tales,* by Maria Cimino. Copyright © 1970 by Maria Cimino. Reprinted by permission of Pantheon Books, a division of Random House, Inc.

page 55, "Nabookin," from *Eurasian Folk and Fairy Tales,* by I. F. Bulatkin. Copyright © 1965 by Criterion Books, Inc. Selection reprinted by permission of HarperCollins Publishers.

page 58, "One Elephant, Deux Éléphants." New lyrics and musical arrangement by Sharon, Lois & Bram. Copyright © 1978 Pachyderm Music. Reprinted by permission.

Selections collected by
Adrienne Betz and Lucia Monfried

Library of Congress Cataloging-in-Publication Data

Diane Goode's book of silly stories & songs / [collected and illustrated] by Diane Goode.—1st ed.

p. cm.

Summary: Presents a collection of humorous folktales and songs, including "The Husband Who Was to Mind the House" and "On Top of Spaghetti."

ISBN 0-525-44967-1

1. Tales. 2. Children's songs—Texts. [1. Folklore. 2. Songs.] I. Goode, Diane.

PZ5.D53 1992

808.8′00083—dc20   91-38192   CIP   AC

Published in the United States by Dutton Children's Books, a division of Penguin Books USA Inc. 375 Hudson Street, New York, New York 10014

Designer: Riki Levinson

Printed in Hong Kong by South China Printing Co.

First Edition   10 9 8 7 6 5 4 3 2 1

Contents

INTRODUCTION

The world is full of such silliness. There does not seem to be a place that is free from it. Someone is always saying or doing a funny thing that makes us laugh. And how wonderful it is to laugh! Laughter is the language everyone understands.

Who can stop themselves from laughing at the foolishness of others? Although it may not be nice, it could be that laughing allows us to feel glad we are where we are, instead of in their shoes. But also, maybe, they remind us—just a *little*—of ourselves. In laughing at them we are able to laugh at our own shortcomings. After all, we could all use a little more common sense. The people in these stories surely need some! They are so very silly. I hope they will make you laugh all the way through this book.

There is a story from Jamaica about why people don't have more common sense. Since it is a silly story, "Getting Common Sense" seems like a good way to begin.

Once upon a time, Anansi thought he would collect all the common sense in the world and keep it for himself.

Anansi started to collect up and collect up all the common sense he could find and put it all into one huge calabash. When he couldn't find any more, Anansi decided to hide his calabash on the top of a very tall tree so that nobody else could reach it.

So Anansi tied a rope around the neck of the calabash and tied the two ends of the rope together and hung the rope around his neck so that the calabash was on his belly. He started up the tall tree, but he couldn't climb very well or very fast because the calabash kept getting in the way. He was trying and trying so hard when all of a sudden he heard a little boy standing on the tree's root burst out laughing. "What a foolish man!" the boy yelled up. "If you want to climb the tree frontways, why don't you put the calabash behind you?"

Well, Anansi was so angry to hear that big piece of common sense coming out of the mouth of such a little boy after he had thought he had collected all the common sense in the world that Anansi took off the calabash and broke it into pieces, and the common sense scattered out in the breeze all over the world. Everybody got a little bit of it, but no one got it all.

THE HUSBAND
WHO WAS TO MIND THE HOUSE
Norwegian

Once there was a man so surly and cross, he never thought his wife did anything much in the house. One evening, he came home scolding and swearing and showing his teeth.

"Dear love, don't be so angry," said his wife. "Tomorrow let's change places. I'll go into the field and mow, and you shall mind the house." The husband thought this was a fine idea and agreed at once.

So early the next morning, his wife took a scythe and went out to work in the field, leaving her husband to work in the house.

The husband began by churning the butter, but the churning made him thirsty and he went down to the cellar to get some ale. Just as he was putting the tap in the cask, he heard a pig come into the kitchen above. He ran up the cellar steps as fast as he could, with the tap in his hand, to catch the pig before it overturned the churn. But by the time he arrived, the pig had already knocked the churn over and was grunting and licking up the cream, which was running all over the floor. The husband was so wild with rage that he forgot the ale barrel and took off after the pig, chasing it from the house. Then he remembered he still had the tap in his hand, but when he got down to the cellar, every drop of ale had run out of the cask.

The husband then went into the dairy and found enough cream left to make butter. So he began to churn. After a while, he remembered that the milking cow was shut up in the cow barn and hadn't had a bite to eat or a drop to drink all morning. So he left the churn and went to the cow barn.

By now the husband was tired, so rather than walk the cow to the meadow, he decided he would just get her up on the housetop, for the house was thatched with sod, and a fine crop of grass was growing on it. The house had a steep hill beside it, and the husband laid a wooden plank across it to the housetop and got the cow up that way. Then he left the cow to graze on the roof.

Now the husband remembered that he had left the churn unattended and his little babe crawling about on the floor. The child is sure to overturn it, he thought. So he put the churn on his back and went outside with it. But then he thought he should first give the cow some water to drink, so he got a bucket to draw water out of the well. But as he stooped down at the edge of the well, all the cream ran out of the churn, over his shoulders, and down into the well.

Now it was getting near dinnertime. The husband hadn't even made the butter, but he thought he'd better begin the porridge. He filled the pot with water and hung it over the fire. When he had done that, he began to wonder if the cow might not fall off the housetop and break her legs or her neck. So he went up on the house to tie her up. He tied one end of the rope to the cow's neck, and the other he slipped down the chimney and tied round his own thigh. He had to make haste, for the water was already boiling in the pot and he still had the oatmeal to grind.

The husband began to grind away. But while he was hard at it,
down fell the cow off the housetop. As she fell, she dragged the
man up the chimney by his leg. There he stuck fast! The cow hung
halfway down the wall, swinging between heaven and earth, for
she could get neither up nor down.

Meanwhile, out in the field, the wife waited for the husband to call her to dinner. Finally she decided she had waited long enough, and she went home. When she got there and saw the cow hanging from the housetop, she ran up and cut the rope in two with her scythe. But as she did, her husband fell down from the chimney. When she came into the kitchen, what did she find? Her husband standing on his head in the porridge pot! And he was very glad to see her back home.

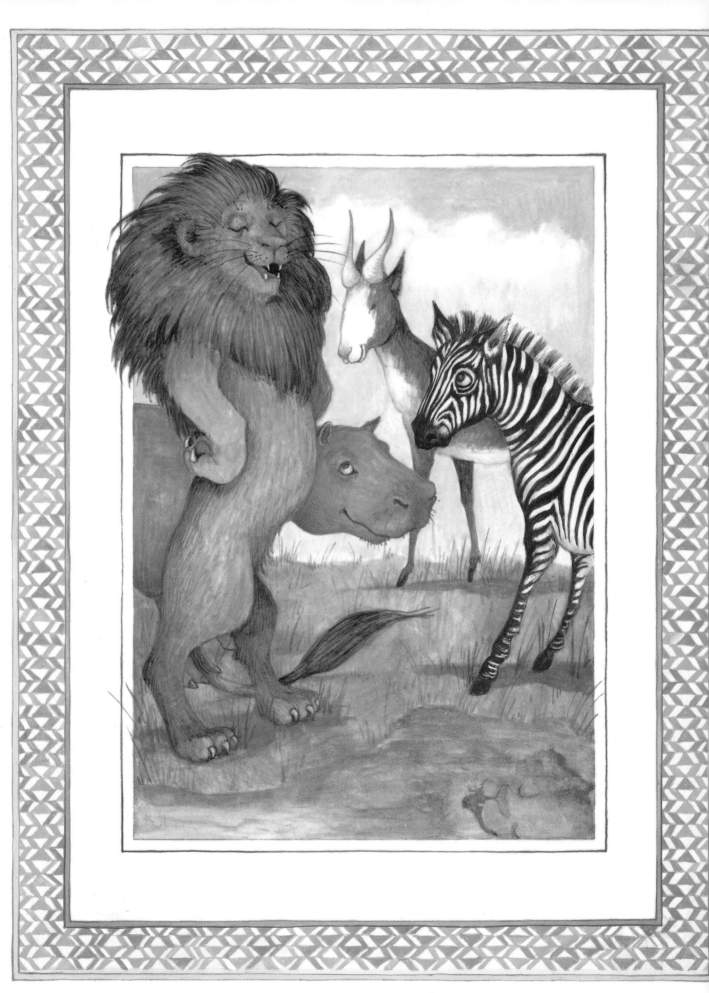

A LION WENT FOR A WALK
African

A lion went for a walk and came upon a small, still pool in which he saw his reflection.

He liked what he saw so much that he decided to find out why the other animals were not as big and strong and beautiful as he was.

The first animal he met was a zebra. "Why is it that you are not as big and strong and beautiful as I am?" he asked. The zebra said he did not know.

The lion then met a hippopotamus and asked him the same question and got the same answer.

Then he met an antelope and asked him, but the antelope did not know either.

Then the lion saw a tiny mouse. "Why is it," he asked, "that you are not as big and strong and beautiful as I am?"

"I've been sick," said the mouse.

GET UP AND BAR THE DOOR
Traditional

nce there lived a couple, a husband and a wife. What kind of people were they? You'll soon find out.

They went to sleep one night and a strong wind came up—a wind that shook the trees and houses. The wind blew their door open.

"Husband," said the wife, "get up and bar the door, for the wind will blow things on our heads."

"You get up. I am tired."

"No. You do it."

"I will not," the silly fellow said.

"I will not," the silly wife said.

So they kept on shouting at each other. They were so deep in their silly argument they never saw a man, a thief, standing at the door, listening to them.

The game kept on, the two blabbering, the wind whistling, and the thief listening, with neither the husband nor the wife getting up to shut the door.

In the end the husband said: "I'll tell you what. I won't talk anymore. It's time you were quiet, too. Let the one who speaks first close the door."

The wife agreed. Each lay in bed, eyes open, lips shut, waiting for the other to speak.

The thief watched them for a while.

"Here's a pair of fools for you," he said to himself. "I will reap the benefit of their folly."

He walked in boldly.

Neither the silly wife nor the silly husband said a word.

"Ha! I can do my work," the thief said aloud.

He took all the things he wanted—clothes, jewels, pots—and made a bundle of them.

Neither the husband nor the wife said a word.

"I must have a little more fun out of this," the thief said.

He went to the fireplace and smeared his hands full of soot. Then he smeared the soot over the man's face, and then over the woman's face.

Neither uttered a word.

The thief walked out the open door.

The man and the wife lay in bed the whole night long, and neither spoke a word.

The sun came up over the village. It was full daylight. Both sat up and looked at each other. The man saw the woman's darkened face; the woman saw the man's darkened face.

She cried out, "Husband, your face is all dark."

"You spoke first," the husband said. "Now you shut the door."

BENDEMOLENA
American

here was once a cat named Bendemolena. She lived in a house where her brothers and sisters, cousins and friends were in and out and all about. What a noisy place it was!

One day Bendemolena found a shiny pot. She put it on her head. Suddenly all the noise was gone. She liked the quiet so much, she decided to wear the pot all the time.

The same day, Mother Cat said to Bendemolena and her brothers and sisters, "I have to take care of a sick friend this afternoon. But, oh, dear! How am I going to clean the house and cook your supper, too?"

"Don't worry," said her kittens. "When you come home, supper will be ready and the house all clean. We'll take care of everything."

Mrs. Cat took Bendemolena with her to the sick friend's house to run errands.

21

"Bendemolena, Bendemolena," said Mrs. Cat, "run home and tell your brothers and sisters that it is time to put the fish on to bake."

Bendemolena didn't hear what her mother said. Her ears were still under the pot. Everything she heard was all mixed up.

"Did she say to put the smish on to fake or to put the bish in the lake?" Bendemolena wondered as she ran home. "Oh! She must have said to put soap in the cake!

"Mama wants you to put soap in the cake," she told her brothers and sisters. All the kittens wanted to please Mother, so they put soap in the cake.

Almost as soon as Bendemolena got back to her mother, Mrs. Cat said, "Bendemolena, Bendemolena, I forgot to tell the children to put the soup on to heat. Run home and tell them to put the soup on to heat."

Again Bendemolena didn't hear very well because of the pot.

"Put the boop on the beep? Mup the moop on the feep? . . . Oh! She must have said to iron the meat!

"Mama says to iron the meat," she told the kittens at home. They all wanted to please Mother, so they got out the iron and ironing board, and ironed the meat.

All afternoon Bendemolena ran back and forth, telling her brothers and sisters what Mother wanted them to do.

Mrs. Cat said, "Bendemolena, Bendemolena, tell them to be sure to leave the key in the lock. Remember, leave the key in the lock."

Bendemolena raced home, saying to herself, "Gleave the bee in the smock? Smick the smee on the sock? Sickee wee wubby gock? . . . Oh! She must have said to sew clothes on the clock.

"Sew clothes on the clock," Bendemolena told her brothers and sisters. And to please their mother, that is what they did.

Bendemolena again ran back to her mother.

"Bendemolena, Bendemolena, supper must be nearly ready. Go tell the children to make something to drink," Mother said.

"Make whiffly sink? Wump buffalo bink? . . . Oh! She must have said to put a horse in the sink!"

When Bendemolena told her brothers and sisters what Mother had said, they asked Mr. Horse, who lived down the street, if he would stand in the sink, just to please their mother.

By this time, animals had come from all over to see for themselves what was happening at Mrs. Cat's house. There were big animals and small animals and in-between-size animals.

Just then Mrs. Cat came home. She saw soap bubbles rising out of the cake. And meat on the ironing board ready to bake. She saw the clock dressed in pink. And a horse in the sink. And then under her chin, ten kittens marched in.

"What is the meaning of this?" Mrs. Cat cried.

"Surprise! Surprise!" said the kittens. They thought they had pleased their mother. They thought they had done just what she wanted. "We all did our best!" they called out.

But Bendemolena was still mixed up. "Ask the rest?" she said to herself. Bendemolena threw open the front door and called, "Everyone come in!"

Mrs. Cat looked at all the neighbors and friends. She looked at Bendemolena's head. Then she looked at her smiling kittens. She just couldn't stay angry. She knew it was all the fault of the pot.

"Everyone can stay for supper," said Mother Cat.

But she took the pot off Bendemolena's head and made two holes for ears in it. Then she put it back on Bendemolena.

"Bendemolena, Bendemolena, give me a hug," said Mrs. Cat.
And did Bendemolena give her mother a bug or a rug?
No! She gave her mother just what she wanted.

CUANTO LE GUSTA

Lyrics by Ray Gilbert
Music by Gabriel Ruiz

Brightly

CHORUS

Cuan - to le gus - ta, le gus - ta, le gus - ta, le

gus - ta, le gus - ta, le gus - ta, le gus - ta, Cuan - to le gus - ta, le

Fine

gus - ta, le gus - ta, le gus - ta, le gus - ta, le gus - ta.

VERSE

We got - ta get go - ing, where're we go - ing? And what are we gon - na
What' - ll we see there, who will be there? And what' - ll be the big sur-

do? We're on our way to some-where, the three of us and you.
prise? There may be se-ñor - i - tas with dark and flash-ing

eyes. We're on our way, _____ pack up your pack, _____
— I'll take a train, _____ you take a boat, _____

____ and if we stay, ____ we won't come back. ____ How can we
____ I'll take a plane, ___ you ride the goat. ___ Oh, we don't

go, _____ we have - n't got a dime. ___ } But we're
care, _____ we'll eith - er walk or climb. ___ }

go - ing and we're going to have a hap - py time. time.

TALK
Ashanti

Once, not far from the city of Accra on the Gulf of Guinea, a country man went out to his garden to dig up some yams to take to market. While he was digging, one of the yams said to him:

"Well, at last you're here. You never weeded me, but now you come around with your digging stick. Go away and leave me alone!"

The farmer turned around and looked at his cow in amazement. The cow was chewing her cud and looking at him.

"Did you say something?" he asked.

The cow kept on chewing and said nothing, but the man's dog spoke up.

"It wasn't the cow who spoke to you," the dog said. "It was the yam. The yam says leave him alone."

The man became angry, because his dog had never talked before, and he didn't like his tone besides. So he took his knife and cut a branch from a palm tree to whip his dog. Just then the palm tree said:

"Put that branch down!"

The man was getting very upset about the way things were going, and he started to throw the palm branch away, but the palm branch said:

"Man, put me down softly!"

He put the branch down gently on a stone, and the stone said:

"Hey, take that thing off me!"

This was enough, and the frightened farmer started to run for his village. On the way he met a fisherman going the other way with a fish trap on his head.

"What's the hurry?" the fisherman asked.

"My yam said, 'Leave me alone!' Then the dog said, 'Listen to what the yam says!' When I went to whip the dog with a palm branch the tree said, 'Put that branch down!' Then the palm branch said, 'Do it softly!' Then the stone said, 'Take that thing off me!'"

"Is that all?" the man with the fish trap asked. "Is that so frightening?"

"Well," the man's fish trap said, "did he take it off the stone?"

"Wah!" the fisherman shouted. He threw the fish trap on the ground and began to run with the farmer, and on the trail they met a weaver with a bundle of cloth on his head.

"Where are you going in such a rush?" he asked them.

"My yam said, 'Leave me alone!'" the farmer said. "The dog said, 'Listen to what the yam says!' The tree said, 'Put that branch down!' The branch said, 'Do it softly!' And the stone said, 'Take that thing off me!'"

"And then," the fisherman continued, "the fish trap said, 'Did he take it off?'"

"That's nothing to get excited about," the weaver said, "no reason at all."

"Oh yes it is," his bundle of cloth said. "If it happened to you you'd run too!"

"Wah!" the weaver shouted. He threw his bundle on the trail and started running with the other men.

They came panting to the ford in the river and found a man bathing.

"Are you chasing a gazelle?" he asked them.

The first man said breathlessly:

"My yam talked at me, and it said, 'Leave me alone!' And my dog said, 'Listen to your yam!' And when I cut myself a branch the tree said, 'Put that branch down!' And the branch said, 'Do it softly!' And the stone said, 'Take that thing off me!'"

The fisherman panted:

"And my trap said, 'Did he?'"

The weaver wheezed:

"And my bundle of cloth said, 'You'd run too!'"

"Is that why you're running?" the man in the river asked.

"Well, wouldn't you run if you were in their position?" the river said.

The man jumped out of the water and began to run with the others. They ran down the main street of the village to the house of the chief. The chief's servants brought his stool out, and he came and sat on it to listen to their complaints. The men began to recite their troubles.

"I went out to my garden to dig yams," the farmer said, waving his arms. "Then everything began to talk! My yam said, 'Leave me alone!' My dog said, 'Pay attention to your yam!' The tree said, 'Put that branch down!' The branch said, 'Do it softly!' And the stone said, 'Take it off me!'"

"And my fish trap said, 'Well, did he take it off?'" the fisherman said.

"And my cloth said, 'You'd run too!'" the weaver said.

"And the river said the same," the bather said hoarsely, his eyes bulging.

The chief listened to them patiently, but he couldn't refrain from scowling.

"Now this is really a wild story," he said at last. "You'd better all go back to your work before I punish you for disturbing the peace."

So the men went away, and the chief shook his head and mumbled to himself, "Nonsense like that upsets the community."

"Fantastic, isn't it?" his stool said. "Imagine, a talking yam!"

THE MISTAKE
Jewish

A rabbi was spending the night at an inn with his students. One of the students had to take an early train. So he asked the innkeeper to wake him at dawn.

The next morning it was pitch-dark when the innkeeper roused him. Careful not to disturb the sleeping rabbi, the student groped in the dark for his clothes. By mistake, he put on the rabbi's long black gabardine gown.

As he hurried through the cold streets to make the train, he wrapped his cloak about him for protection, never noticing the error he had made.

When he arrived at the station, the pious student stopped short before his own reflection in the station mirror. He stared at the long black gown.

"What an idiot that innkeeper is!" he exclaimed in anger. "I asked him to wake me, and instead he woke the rabbi!"

ON TOP OF SPAGHETTI

Tom Glazer

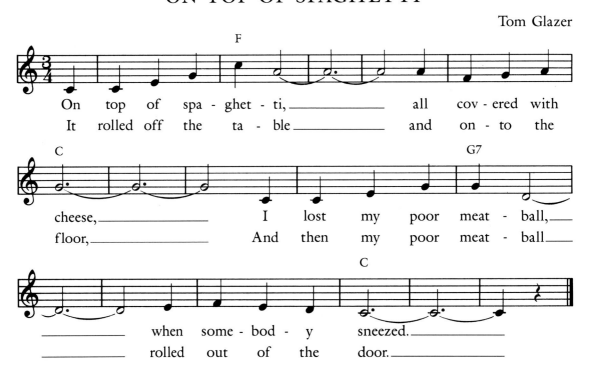

On top of spa-ghet-ti, _____ all cov-ered with cheese, _____ I lost my poor meat-ball, _____ when some-bod-y sneezed. _____

It rolled off the ta-ble _____ and on-to the floor, _____ And then my poor meat-ball _____ rolled out of the door. _____

It rolled in the garden
and under a bush,
And then my poor meatball
was nothing but mush.

The mush was as tasty
as tasty could be,
And early next summer
it grew into a tree.

The tree was all covered
with beautiful moss,
It grew lovely meatballs
and tomato sauce.

So if you eat spaghetti,
all covered with cheese,
Hold on to your meatballs
and don't ever sneeze.

TINGALAYO

Calypso

CHORUS

Ting - a - lay - o! Come, lit - tle don - key come. Ting - a -
lay - o! Come, lit - tle don - key come.

VERSE

Me don-key hee, me don-key haw, Me don-key sleep on— a bed of straw.
Me don-key walk, me don-key talk, Me don-key eat with— a knife and fork.

After each of the following verses, repeat the chorus.

Me donkey eat, me donkey sleep,
Me donkey kick with his two hind feet.

Me donkey laugh, me donkey cry,
Me donkey love peanut butter pie.

SWEET GIONGIO
Southern Italian

There once was a sensible young man who fell in love with a pretty young woman. Her father was only too happy to give her hand in marriage to the man. The woman's family held a splendid wedding, and relatives came from miles around.

During the wedding feast the bride went to the wine cellar for a special bottle of *vin santo* that had been saved for just such an occasion. But as she was about to pull the wine bottle from the rack, she noticed a piece of broken glass on the floor. She sat down on the cellar steps and burst out in tears.

"Within a year, God willing, I will have a son. And he will grow into a curious little boy. I'll name him Giongio Cippolone. And what if sweet Giongio should go into the wine cellar to play and find a piece of glass like this and, being the curious soul that he is, pick it up and, being just a small child, fall and, being most unlucky, cut his throat!" The young bride wept and wept.

Upstairs, the bride's mother began to wonder what was keeping her daughter. So she went down to the cellar and found her daughter in tears.

"Ah, Mama. I found this piece of glass," said the bride. "What if my son Giongio five years from now should come into this cellar and get cut and die!"

"Oh, no. My poor grandson Giongio." And the bride's mother burst out in tears.

Next it was the bride's father's turn to see what was keeping them. When he heard the story, he said, "Poor sweet lost Giongio." And he burst out in tears.

Next came the brothers and sisters of the bride. Then the cousins, fourteen of them. And the aunts and uncles and grandparents. Soon the wine cellar was overflowing with wailing relatives.

When nobody returned, the groom went to the cellar to find his bride. But the cellar was so full he had to stand at the top of the stairs and shout down to her. "What on earth is going on?" he yelled. When he heard why they were all crying, he threw his hands into the air. "I have married into a family of crazy folk," he said. "Everyone said you were silly, but I had no idea how bad it was! I'm leaving now and going out into the world. And I won't come back unless I find three people sillier than you." With that, the groom marched off.

He walked along until he reached a river. There he saw a farmer watering two oxen with a spoon—first one, then the other.

"Whatever are you doing?" asked the groom.

"I've been here for three hours and can't seem to quench these animals' thirst."

"Why not let them put their muzzles in the water?" asked the groom.

"Their muzzles in the water? What a marvelous idea!" said the farmer. "How brilliant you are!"

Silly number one, thought the groom, and he continued on his way until dusk deepened into night. Feeling tired, the groom decided to sleep outside. No sooner had he settled himself beside a lake than a voice cried, "Oh, no, it's happened again!"

The groom got up and saw a man at the edge of the lake scooping a fishnet through the water over and over again. "Oh, no," said the man. "Oh, no. Oh, no."

"Whatever are you doing?" asked the groom.

"The moon has fallen into the lake," said the man. "I must save her before she drowns."

"Look," said the groom, pointing at the sky. "There's the moon right up there where she should be. What you see in the water is nothing more than her reflection."

"Oh," said the man, looking from the moon to the water and back again. "Oh, yes, I see. How brilliant you are!"

Silly number two, thought the groom. Then he got up and went to the nearest inn so he could get a good night's sleep.

In the morning the groom woke to banging sounds on the ceiling above his bed. He climbed the stairs and opened the door to the room over his. There he saw the innkeeper and his wife. The wife held the innkeeper's trousers out in front of her. The innkeeper ran across the room and jumped at the trousers, knocking his wife to the floor.

"Whatever are you doing?" asked the groom.

"Trousers are so difficult to put on, don't you think?" said the innkeeper. "I've been trying to jump into mine for the last half hour. It sometimes takes me a whole hour to get them on."

"Have you tried sitting on the bed and pulling them on?" asked the groom.

"Sitting on the bed?" exclaimed the man. "Yes, yes, I think that might work. How brilliant you are!"

That makes three, thought the groom. It seemed to him that the world was full of silly people.

And so he went back home to his wife. In good time they had a son and named him Giongio Cippolone. But Giongio did not die. He still lives happily with his mother and father.

THE MAGIC POT
Traditional

There was once a poor but good little girl who lived alone with her mother. They were so poor that they had nothing to eat. The little girl was so hungry that she went into the forest to look for food. There she met an old woman. The old woman felt sorry for the girl and gave her a pot. "Whenever you want porridge, say, 'Cook, little pot, cook,'" the old woman told the girl. And the pot would cook good sweet porridge.

The child took the pot home to her mother, and they were no longer hungry. They ate good sweet porridge whenever they wished.

One day the little girl went out and her mother said, "Cook, little pot, cook." The pot cooked, and the mother ate until she was full. Then she wanted the pot to stop cooking, but she forgot the words to make it stop. The little girl knew the words, but she was not at home. So the pot went right on cooking, and the porridge bubbled over the top.

It cooked and cooked until the kitchen was full of porridge, and the whole house was full of porridge, and then the next house, and then the whole street. The pot kept right on cooking and cooking. Everyone in town wanted the pot to stop cooking, but no one knew how to do it.

At last, when only one house remained that was not covered with porridge, the little girl came home. She said, "Stop, little pot, stop." And it stopped.

The townspeople all looked at one another and shook their heads. And whoever wanted to return to town had to eat his way back.

THE DISOBEDIENT EELS
Venetian

One day a fisherman from Chioggia came to Venice with a basketful of eels. Wanting to get across a canal, he asked what the fare was.

"Five cents a head," said the ferryman.

"Oh, that's too much for all these heads," said the fisherman, looking at his basket. "Into the water, my dear eels. It's swimming across for you. I'll wait on the other side."

He emptied his basket into the canal, paid his fare, and was across in no time. Then he sat down on the landing to wait for his eels.

He waited, calling out now and then, "Hey, eels! Where are you? Why are you so long in getting here? Come on, swim this way!"

And gondoliers say that he is still sitting there, waiting for his eels.

NABOOKIN
Iranian

ne day Nabookin cooked a pot of rice and roasted a fat chicken. But as he wasn't very hungry, he thought he would go for a walk and work up a real appetite.

So Nabookin left the food on the table, locked his door, put the key under a stone, and went for a walk. As he was walking along the road he met two young men. Looking at them suspiciously, he asked, "Where are you going, you rascals?"

The passersby stared at him in amazement.

"Aha! You don't answer!" exclaimed Nabookin. "You rogues are going to eat my dinner. There stands my house, and in my room I have left rice and a fat chicken. I have locked the house and put the key under the big stone that lies in front of the door . . . but if you eat my rice and chicken I will drag you before the judge." And shaking his fist in the air he turned and went on his way.

At first the young men took him for a fool and did not believe him. But passing Nabookin's house they saw a stone in front of the door. One of them, merely out of curiosity, lifted the stone, and what did he see? The key!

They opened the door and there on the table was the rice and roast chicken. The dish looked so tempting that they could not resist it and fell to eating with gusto, leaving poor Nabookin one well-gnawed carcass. Then they left, locking the house and putting the key in its old place under the stone.

After a long walk Nabookin returned home hungry, his mouth watering at the thought of the delicious rice and roast chicken. He took the key from under the stone and opened the door. On the table he saw the carcass, picked clean.

He began to howl like a savage and stretched out on the floor in grief. Then he got up, sat down near the plate, and thought, "Who ate my dinner? If I had not found the key in its place, I could say that those boys ate it, but the key is still under the stone, so it is impossible to accuse them."

Suddenly he saw a fly buzz around and then light on the gnawed bones. Nabookin held his breath and, sneaking up to it, managed to capture the fly. It tried to escape and started to buzz. Nabookin became furious.

"How can you do this?" he cried. "You ate my rice and chicken and now you make fun of me by buzzing! I insist on justice. I will drag you before the judge."

Nabookin set off to the judge with the fly in his hand, demanding justice against the fly who had eaten his rice and chicken.

The judge was glad of the chance to make fun of this fool.

"In the Book of Allah it says that you must let the fly go and strike it with a stick. If you hit it, that means the fly is guilty. But if you miss, that means it is innocent." The judge gave Nabookin a stout stick.

Nabookin freed the fly. The fly buzzed and buzzed and then settled on the judge's nose. Nabookin swung the stick with all his might. The fly flew up to the ceiling—and the judge toppled to the floor. On his nose a huge lump arose.

"Apparently the fly is not guilty," said Nabookin, and departed for home.

The judge rubbed his nose and groaned, "Oh, Allah, truly one should try to teach a fool, not laugh at him."

ONE ELEPHANT, DEUX ÉLÉPHANTS

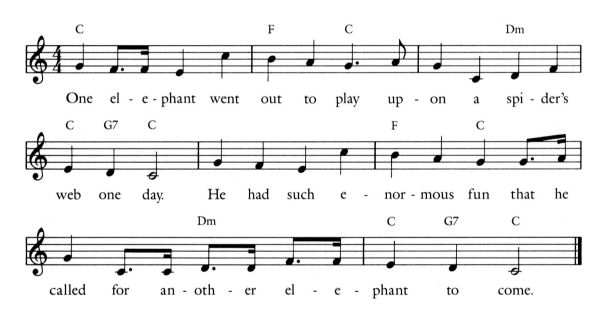

One el - e - phant went out to play up - on a spi - der's web one day. He had such e - nor - mous fun that he called for an - oth - er el - e - phant to come.

Deux éléphants allaient jouer
Sur une toile d'araignée.
Ils s'amusaient tellement bien
Qu'ils appelaient à un autre, viens!

Three elephants went out to play
Upon a spider's web one day.
They had such enormous fun
That they called for another elephant
  to come.

Quatre éléphants allaient jouer
Sur une toile d'araignée.
Ils s'amusaient tellement bien
Qu'ils appelaient à un autre, viens!

All the elephants were out at play
Upon a spider's web one day.
They had such enormous fun
But there were no more elephants left
  to come.

MICHAEL FINNEGAN

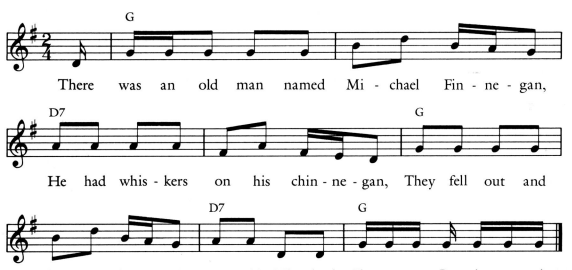

There was an old man named Michael Finnegan,
He had whiskers on his chinnegan,
They fell out and then grew in again,
Poor old Michael Finnegan, Begin again.

There was an old man named
   Michael Finnegan,
He grew fat and then grew thin again,
Then he died and had to begin again,
Poor old Michael Finnegan,
Begin again.

There was an old man named
   Michael Finnegan,
He went fishing with a pinnegan,
Caught a fish and dropped it in again,
Poor old Michael Finnegan,
Begin again.

MASTER OF ALL MASTERS
English

girl once went to the fair to hire herself out as a servant. At last a funny-looking old gentleman engaged her and took her to his house. When she got there, he told her that he had something to teach her, for in his house he had his own names for things.

He said to her: "What will you call me?"

"Master or mister, or whatever you please, sir," she said.

He said: "You must call me 'Master of all masters.' And what would you call this?" he demanded, pointing to his bed.

"Bed or couch, or whatever you please, sir."

"No, that's my 'barnacle.' And what do you call these?" said he, pointing to his pantaloons.

"Breeches or trousers, or whatever you please, sir."

"You must call them 'squibs and crackers.' And what would you call her?" he asked, pointing to the cat.

"Cat or kit, or whatever you please, sir."
"You must call her 'white-faced simminy.' And this now," showing the fire, "what would you call this?"

"Fire or flame, or whatever you please, sir."
"You must call it 'hot cockalorum.' And what about this?" he went on, pointing to the water.

"Water or wet, or whatever you please, sir."
"No, 'pondalorum' is its name. And what do you call all this?" asked he, as he pointed to the house.

"House or cottage, or whatever you please, sir."
"You must call it 'high topper mountain.'"

That very night the servant woke her master up in a fright and said: "Master of all masters, get out of your barnacle and put on your squibs and crackers. For white-faced simminy has got a spark of hot cockalorum on her tail, and unless you get some pondalorum, high topper mountain will be all on hot cockalorum."
...... That's all.

SOURCE NOTES

GETTING COMMON SENSE Anansi, a famous trickster figure, is both man and spider. Stories about him originated in West Africa and were brought to Jamaica and the Caribbean with the Africans, where they were passed down through generations. Usually Anansi is the clever one, but at times he is shown up, as in this story.

THE HUSBAND WHO WAS TO MIND THE HOUSE Originally from Norway, this favorite story of vocational turnabout, with the wife coming out the better of her arrogant but hapless husband, was printed in *Popular Tales from the Norse,* by Peter Christian Asbjörnsen and Jörgen Moe (1888). In Scandinavia alone, nearly two hundred variants of this story have been collected.

A LION WENT FOR A WALK This type of tale—long and convoluted, with a conclusion that is absurd—is known as a shaggy-dog story. Alvin Schwartz notes that different animals appear in variants of this story; a five-thousand-year-old version from Sumer has the final dialogue between an elephant and a wren.

GET UP AND BAR THE DOOR M. A. Jagendorf's two collections of numskull, or noodlehead, stories, *Noodlehead Stories from Around the World* and *More Noodlehead Stories from Around the World,* are invaluable resources for this type of tale. Jagendorf notes that he found over twenty versions of this popular tale from as many different lands. A song version also exists, whose text is very close to an early Scottish variant, from 1769.

BENDEMOLENA The authors draw on a traditional device used in children's games and folktales in which misunderstood words and garbled speech lead to humorous misunderstandings.

TALK is based on a story heard in Nigeria by Harold Courlander from an Ashanti from the Gold Coast. Courlander, a preeminent folklorist and authority on the oral literature of Africa, is the author of over twenty books, including *A Treasury of African Folklore,* an extensive collection covering the widespread regions of the African continent.

THE MISTAKE is one of a body of stories about the legendary shtetl of Chelm, in Poland, all of whose inhabitants are fools. Like the Gothamites in England, they are known the world over for their collective, innocent stupidity. Nathan Ausubel, in his authoritative collection *A Treasury of Jewish Folklore,* notes that there is no body of humorous folk literature more widely disseminated among Yiddish-speaking Jews than the stories about these fools, and that the tales typify Jewish irony and wit.

SWEET GIONGIO is a variant of the "Three Sillies" story, the most enduring and widespread of drolls, or numskull stories. Called "Clever Else" by the Grimms (Grimm 34), this story type is found in all parts of Europe, as well as in Siberia, and has parallels in Africa. A Roman version, called "Cicco Petrillo," was collected by Italo Calvino in *Italian Folk Tales,* while the Venetian variant, called "Bastienelo," was collected by Virginia Haviland in *Told in Italy. Giongio* is a common southern Italian name, and *Cippolone* means "onion head."

THE MAGIC POT is a variant of a story collected by Jacob and Wilhelm Grimm called "Sweet Porridge" (Grimm 103). Sometimes known as "The Wonderful Porridge Pot," it appears in Carolyn S. Bailey's classic collection for American librarians and storytellers, *For the Children's Hour,* published by Milton Bradley in 1906.

THE DISOBEDIENT EELS Maria Cimino, the former head of the Central Children's Room of the New York Public Library and a noted storyteller, collected many of the stories in her book *The Disobedient Eels and Other Italian Tales* from the Marciana Library in Venice.

NABOOKIN According to the five duties of Islam, every Muslim must make a pilgrimage to Mecca. On the roads to Mecca, Muslims from many nations passed the time exchanging news and folktales. Twelve centuries of this pilgrimage, the *hajj,* has yielded a rich folklore throughout the Muslim world. This Iranian tale is typical of Muslim stories, which often include some sort of moral. The fly-chasing element is pure slapstick, recognizable in comedy from many cultures.

MASTER OF ALL MASTERS was printed in the seminal collection *English Fairy Tales,* collected by Joseph Jacobs (1898). Jacobs comments in his notes that he took what suited him for his version from a number of sources, "which shows how widespread this quaint droll is in England." The humor comes from the brevity of the story as compared to the girl's long-winded, nonsensical answer, and from the demanding master getting his comeuppance.